A Leap of FAITH

LINDA BOULANGER

A Coin in the Fountain Love Story

A Leap of Faith
©2017 by Linda Boulanger

Edited by Grace Augustine/Edits with a Touch of Grace
Cover Design/Interior Design by Tell~Tale Book Covers
First released as part of the The Fountain Box Set

Published by TreasureLine Publishing

Also available in eBook publication

PRINTED IN THE UNITED STATES OF AMERICA

To Mom...
Thank you for giving me the courage
to take my own leap of faith.

Chapter 1

The sun glistened off the rippling water in the fountain and cast a shadow over the face of the dragon statue standing guard in the center. A different kind of shadow shrouded the young woman who stood at the edge of the pool. Knees slightly bent, she leaned forward, laboring to pull in great gulps of air. She cocked her head, coppery red curls sliding from her back, swishing against the cotton fabric of her dress as she tried to listen for noise beyond the drumming between her ears. Her heart sank. She could still hear the sound of feet slapping against the earth, way too close for her to gain any comfort from the distance.

Sucking in another deep breath, she straightened and shook her head trying to clear her mind. She needed to think, especially since none of what was happening made any sense.

"Come on, Rynne," she chided herself, knowing she also needed to hurry. If those men caught her, she might never get home.

Eyelids closing over deep blue orbs, she prayed the old gypsy woman was right. This had to work, otherwise… Rynne Willowthorne shivered. She couldn't bring herself to think of the otherwise. Instead, she concentrated on the words the dark-skinned woman with even darker hair and eyes had told her.

The Gypsy had made her repeat them multiple times after giving her the coin when she'd slipped into her shoppe in an attempt to avoid the men.

Her lips curled into the beginnings of a curse directed at the old witch back home who had sent her forward in time. Thinking better of it, she bit her tongue, quickly clamping her mouth shut. Had it not been for the witch, she wouldn't have the potion to help her brother.

Provided he wasn't already dead, her inner voice whispered.

Rynne growled. He wasn't dead. But in that perpetual sleep he fell into after he put on the ring from their father, he might as well be.

That's why she'd swallowed her fears and had gone to the old witch for help in the first place. She sighed, remembering how the woman had taken two steps away from her, crossed herself, and shook her head with such fervor that Rynne was concerned it might snap right off her thin neck.

It was all quite comical really. She'd nearly laughed, catching herself just in time to keep from it. She'd needed the woman's help, not to find herself on the receiving end of one of the spells she knew the witch was capable of.

From across the room, the old hag told her to go to the Cave of Dracha where she would find a pool of water. Rynne was to take the heart-shaped vial the bony finger pointed to on a shelf against the far wall and fill it with the water. It sounded so simple she was sure that even she could do it. Only, when she leaned forward, she fell in. She could have sworn she'd been pushed, but that was neither here nor there. The fact was, she'd gone into the water in the cave and when she'd surfaced, a clear blue sky had hung above her head and it had taken her all of four seconds to realize the sky was in a time not her own. The huge shiny bird reminded her of the blade of a sword. It flew far above her, initially confusing her, but it was the woman at the water's edge who had finally made her understand.

The woman motioned for Rynne to follow, even before her feet touched solid ground.

"Come. I have what you need."

Rynne's heart beat faster than she'd imagined possible. She crawled from the water and followed at a distance, surprised the woman never once looked over her shoulder to see if she was back there. She'd probably been able to hear Rynne slogging behind in her sodden clothing. Walking in a wet dress would have been bad enough, but three layers… She'd never hated the thickness of her kirtle more.

Her need outweighing her fear, she finally stammered out the one question that she probably should have asked from the beginning.

"Where am I?"

The woman answered with the name of a place Rynne had never heard of, supplying the year as well. She chuckled when Rynne gasped.

Had Rynne not just surfaced in a different place than the one she had fallen in, she would never have believed she could've fallen over five hundred years into the future. It wasn't possible... and yet, it had happened.

Rynne's heart raced, her mind searching for a way to keep from having to continue this crazy journey. She wondered, or maybe hoped that she would wake up and find it all a dream. She pressed her eyes tightly shut for a few seconds and pinched herself as she opened them. The sights, the smells... they remained distinctly not her own.

A hound came running toward them when they crested the next hill, and Rynne could see a house nestled in the trees not far beyond. She was glad because the ache in her legs and the growling of her stomach were pushing primal need before fear. She frowned. She'd eaten just before going to visit the old witch. It may have seemed to have taken mere seconds, but her trip through time must have lasted much longer.

When the woman stopped at the bottom of the steps that led to the door of the house, she reached down to pet the dog and Rynne realized it was no dog at all. It was a black wolf.

Rynne held her distance, even though the animal showed no intent to harm. Much like the hounds back home at Honorcrest, the beast gazed up at its master with great admiration, especially when her fingers reached that magical spot just behind his ears.

"He's harmless," the woman told her, almost as if she could read her thoughts. "Unless I want him to be otherwise."

The combination of her chuckle and the deep

throatiness of her voice made goosebumps rise on Rynne's arms. There was something different about her.

"Go, Vilks," she ordered the black beast. "Stand watch."

Rynne could have sworn the wolf bowed his head before he turned and took off. As quickly as he went, she wondered if magic had taken him away.

"Come," the woman commanded her, much as she had the wolf. She stopped at the threshold of the doorway and looked out across the land, squinting as she did so. "There's not much time," she told her. "Your presence here has alerted many. They're already looking for you."

Her eyes going wide, Rynne looked over her shoulder to see no signs that anyone was near. Still, she shot up the steps to join the woman, blinking as she walked into the interior of the dusky cottage. She shivered, a feeling of movement in the dark shadows making her skin crawl. But it was the vial next to a low burning candle in the middle of a table that grabbed her attention. It was exactly like the one she'd lost in the pool, except for the murky liquid inside. When she reached for it, the woman stopped her. Rynne turned determined eyes upward meeting those of the taller woman. All fear aside, she had to have that vial.

After a few seconds, the woman broke the stare and smiled.

"Mordrin was right. You are a strong one."

Rynne gasped at the mention of the name of the old witch back home.

"I am Corvona Bruxa." She laughed again at Rynne's raised brows. "I see you've heard of the Raven Witch. Don't worry. I mostly use my magic for good these days." She cooed as she pulled a thin ball chain from a rack hanging above the table, working it through the eyelet screw in the top of the bottle top.

"Wickedness can get so tiresome as one ages, especially in this day when it is so plentiful. It's much more fun now to foil the nefarious."

Rynne scrutinized the woman while she worked with the bottle. A few inches taller than herself, she couldn't imagine her being more than a decade older than she was, which was odd because the fabled Raven Witch had supposedly lived centuries before her own time.

Her lithe body was clad in black from knee high boots to her leather pants, even the vest that covered her dark shirt was black, as was her hair and eyes. It was easy to see why she was called the Raven. When she handed her the vial, Rynne jumped and the woman laughed again. She could tell some of the witch's old ways still remained.

"You needed a better way of securing it," she told her, motioning for Rynne to put the chain over her head. "Now, for a change of clothes. Those wet skirts will slow you down too much."

Too much for what, Rynne wondered.

Rynne had just managed to change when the wolf bayed and the dark-haired witch told her the men had come. She handed her a black feather and told her to run, to find the water, and that the coin would assure her return home.

And run Rynne had, back in the direction she thought they'd come. The problem was, there was no water, only a town. Secondly, or maybe it was the third problem, since she was now being pursued, was that she had no coin.

Believe, her inner voice told her.

She had to believe everything would work out. She couldn't lose hope. It was all she had to save her brother's life.

"Slow down," she whispered to herself at the edge of the town.

Rynne forced herself to return a smile to a lady who walked past with an infant in an odd-looking carriage. Making herself take slower steps while trying to control her breathing, she walked into the town trying to figure out what to do next.

Part of her screamed that she needed to turn back, but she could hear runners in the distance and assumed they were the men the Raven Witch had told her about. She still had no idea who they were or how they'd known she was there, but she felt certain they wanted the vial.

Rynne's heart sank. She didn't know where she was or how she was going to get the potion home to her brother, provided she could avoid the men chasing her. She'd needed to find the water, not a town with oddly constructed buildings along even odder streets.

What material looked of white dirt, yet felt as hard as wood beneath one's feet?

She looked up, squinting at the lights that hung from black posts above her. The same kind of light shone in the windows of the shoppes, but it wasn't from oil lamps or candlelight. It illumined clothing that looked more like undergarments than outer attire. It was like nothing she'd ever seen, what with the short length of the women's skirts and the tight form of the men's britches. Scandal would have erupted had people dressed this way back in her brother's fiefdom of Wolfdenreve.

A call came from behind her and she whipped around to see four men, one of them pointing toward her. They had to be the ones who had been following her.

Dressed in the same odd clothing of the other villagers, they quickly blended in and Rynne knew she had to get away. She took off, darting down a side street, weaving through an alley and into a shoppe that looked to sell items closer to what she might have seen at home. Inside, the old Gypsy woman seemed to be expecting her and held out a heavily bangled arm, hand upward, asking for the raven feather only seconds after Rynne burst through the door. Rynne looked at the black feather Corvona Bruxa had given her. Was this the reason why? What if she gave it up and…

When the Gypsy woman produced a coin in her other hand, Rynne thrust the feather at her and grabbed the coin.

"Where?"

The gypsy understood her one-word question and replied, "To the fountain with the dragon's body," she answered.

Rynne leaned closer, trying to understand through the woman's thick accent and clipped words.

"Say these words and step into the water." The Gypsy recited a handful of words, had Rynne repeat them, then took Rynne to a door in the back of the shoppe that let her out into yet another alley. "Stay to the East, with the sun before you."

Rynne thanked her and ran until she found the fountain exactly where the woman had said it would be. Slowing as she approached it, she stared at it, circling it, and taking in the design. Quite old looking, it was magnificent with the water trickling from the stone dragon's mouth into the basin atop the pedestal that rose from the center to where it then cascaded down into a coin-strewn pool. It appeared to be constructed of a fine stone, except for the tile bottom and the copper eyes.

With shaky legs, she climbed up on the fountains edge, feeling ludicrous when she spread her arms like the woman had told her, and even more so when she turned three times and began chanting the words she'd been rehearsing in her mind.

"Întoarce-mă la mine acasă."

Rynne wasn't quite sure of their meaning, only that when she combined them with the actions and tossed the ancient coin into the fountain, they were supposed to take her from this place, sweeping her through time. She prayed for safety.

Even though she'd crossed time before, fear still crept up her spine. This time she was doing it on purpose. She second-guessed herself. What if something else went wrong and she ended up God only knew where?

Mustering as much courage as she possibly could, Rynne lifted her chin and braced herself, knowing she was the only hope her brother had. Now, with the vial secured on a chain that allowed it to hang low, nestled in the hollow between her breasts, she had to get back home where she could help him.

With the words completed, Rynne kissed the coin and tossed it toward the stone beast in the middle and stepped forward. Before either she or the coin landed, she could feel herself falling… floating, really. This time, she submitted to it, allowing herself to be pulled in, whisked away on the threads of time like a soft feather sailing upon the wind.

"Home," she whispered.

Rynne was ready to be home. She had to believe her wish would come true. She *had* to believe, because this was her only chance.

Chapter 2

All Brendan MacCailín wanted was a few extra minutes of peace outside his bedchamber. That seemed to be the only place he could be alone anymore. He stood near the pond at the far end of his garden, breathing in the familiar smells of his own lands. The gentle breeze that ruffled his brown hair was welcomed.

He'd ordered the windows of his castle opened to take advantage of the reprieve from the stillness of the days prior. The air had grown quite stale within his halls during his time away, especially since his sisters had refused to allow the windows opened.

His Steward had done his best to wrought compliance from them, but they'd refused to listen to the man. Poor Durstan, a man in his middle ages who had never married, he'd been content to spend his life acting as Steward to Locktonhurst. Running the castle was the man's forte, not corralling young women on the verge of becoming headstrong ladies.

Three months they'd held Brendan's home captive, demanding the windows locked after the first of the feathers had been found. Three months, plus travel time, adding another six days was how long he'd been gone.

He hadn't been away that long since his years

spent at the Battle of Volante. He'd been ready to come home, until Sophia met him at the door blubbering about the black feathers they'd been finding in various places inside his halls.

Brendan had rubbed his shoulder, the hair on the back of his neck standing up at the mention of the black feathers, though the concern was quickly replaced with a sense of right. Whether that was because he was home, or the strange happenings were a foretelling of something good, he wasn't sure. One thing was certain, the black feathers meant something. Not only had they been found in his home, but one had also emerged as a dark scale-like image on the flesh of his right shoulder. It was his mark. He'd been expecting it, even if he hadn't known what it would look like.

He shuddered. Change was upon them. Too bad his sisters couldn't embrace it.

Unfortunately, with the unrest in the neighboring fiefdom of Thurwickden, everyone was on edge and they couldn't accept that whatever was happening just might bring good. He groaned, knowing he needed to do some accepting of his own. It could be a good while before they stopped shadowing him.

Brendan rubbed his shoulder. He needed time to think, to figure out what was happening. More importantly, he needed to find out what his part was in the whole of things. If only he could arrange for Sophia and Margaret to visit elsewhere. He loved his sisters, but their continual care since his parent's passing was quite wearisome even in the best of times.

And this was not necessarily the best of times. He touched the spot on his shoulder, thinking of his recent trip. It had come at the request of the mother of his best friend, Kensey Willowthorne. Lord of Honorcrest in the fiefdom of Wolfdenreve, Willowthorne had taken ill and his younger sister had gone missing.

Brendan sighed. He hadn't seen his friend in almost a year, though the last time they'd been together he'd thought Kensey fit enough. It was strange to see the man laying abed as if asleep though never waking, his only nourishment coming from whatever liquid his mother could force past his lips. The cream on the milk had come with his sister's disappearance... this was the main reason Kensey's mother had summoned him... to lead the men in a search for her.

Lady Katrynne, he'd been told, was closer in age to his sister Margaret than she was to himself or Kensey. He'd never met the girl and could scarce imagine the coppery-red hair and blue eyes that had been described, especially given the more brunette coloring of both Kensey and his mother.

The younger brother, Vander, came closer to what he'd imagined she would look like, though his hair was a faded blonde and his eyes so pale they could scarce be called blue.

He couldn't fathom her being much to look at, but her family had asked, offering a handsome purse for her return. Brendan hadn't been interested in the purse so much as he was doing this favor for his friend's family. He owed Willowthorne his life, at least thrice over.

But he hadn't been able to find the girl.

Brendan kicked a rock on the pathway beside the water. So many days and nights spent searching, following every lead remotely plausible... and even a few that had not been. A trip to the old witch, Mordrin, had been the last straw. She'd told them about a cave where they'd found the girl's cloak rocking back and forth in the foamy water that lapped the rocks at the edge of the pool.

He shook his head. The hag had cackled when they'd returned to confront her, telling them the girl was *one of them*, that she'd *seen her dragon*, but that the only way for her to help them was if the girl went forward. Her prattling made no sense but it was all he could get out of the old witch. Even when he'd threatened to run her through, she'd just laughed.

Mordrin had walked off, spouting that death would be a welcomed friend to one who had lived a thousand lifetimes. They could hear her in the distance mumbling about weary bones and missing teeth.

It was after that final visit that the mark had appeared on his skin. He'd also felt the stirring of the beast inside, something he'd known would come, and he knew his days as a mere man were coming to a close. With his hand dropping down to feel the mass in the bag at his waist, he turned to head back to the castle, surprised his sisters had given him this long alone.

Brendan had taken no more than two steps when he felt the hair on the back of his neck stand up and his palm went to the hilt of his sword. He spun around, his eyes widening as a loud splash shot water toward the sky. The sound of sputtering and coughing followed a head bobbing above the water's surface. Brendan gasped. Not just any head, it was that of a woman... a copper-headed beauty that took his breath away as she gained her footing and stood.

Slinging water from her fingertips, the vision slogged from the pond, her eyes as big as his.

"Wh... where am I?" she managed through another round of coughing.

When he didn't answer, she lifted her brow, her lips pursing as she reached down to wring a puddle of water from the front of her dress. She straightened, shaking her hands again as she let her gaze slide down him, then glanced over his shoulder at his castle then back at him, a hopeful smile lighting still wary eyes.

"I'm guessing I've at least made it home, though I'm not quite sure where," she mumbled more to herself than to him. "I'll also presume you aren't foe for you have yet to run me through."

They both looked at his hand still on the hilt of his sheathed sword.

"N... no," he fumbled with his words. "Uhm..." When his gaze kept dropping, she looked down then squinted at him with her mouth open, her nose crinkled in disgust. She sucked in, crossing her arms over her chest and motioned for him to turn around.

Brendan almost laughed, though he did as she asked. He may be a hot-blooded male, but he was also a gentleman, warranted by his societal position. Damn society. He'd much rather ogle the perfect curves highlighted beneath her wet gown.

"Perhaps you could at least offer a Lady your tabard?"

Brendan raised a brow and pursed his lips as he glanced over his shoulder, her glare causing him to again look away.

"Supposing I am indeed dealing with a Lady, I assume that would be the proper thing to do."

He had to bite his lower lip when he heard her growl. Chuckling, he stammered an apology before shirking out of his sleeveless jacket and tossing it in her direction, listening for the telltale signs that she'd managed to work it over her head before he turned back around.

"Are you lord of this castle?" she asked.

Brendan couldn't help but be a little amused at the color that had crept into her cheeks as their moments together had progressed.

She was a pretty woman, even with her coppery red curls flattened against her head from her dunk in his pond. Her eyes reminded him of the tranquility of a deep blue stream on a still day, though they were anything but peaceful.

Even filled with unmistakable caution, a dark fire danced within their depths, warming Brendan from the inside and he had to stop himself from smiling at the thought of how they might look staring up at him as she writhed beneath him... Heavens! It had obviously been far too long since he'd been with a woman since he was having feelings like he was so quickly after making her acquaintance... though he really hadn't made her acquaintance yet, had he? What the hell was happening? He narrowed his gaze. Was she bewitching him?

Clearing his throat forcefully and standing taller, he finally answered.

"I am. And if you don't mind, *my lady*, I would have your name, as well as an answer to how you came to be in my pond, lest I call my guard and have you escorted to the highest room in my tower."

Chapter 3

Rynne stopped adjusting the tabard over her wet clothing and gave the man her full attention. Was he serious? She cocked her head, scrutinizing him, trying to discern an answer. His dark blue eyes held censure and there was no doubt he was a man of authority. Handsome beyond words, simply gazing at the lord of this castle had set her senses reeling, her heart to racing.

Thoughts that didn't belong in the head of a proper lady swirled through her mind and, for a moment, she imagined running her fingers through the brown waves that covered his head. They were a bit unruly, though she thought the wildness suited him, as did the scruff that speckled his jaw and chin. There was something almost feral about him.

His hand tightening around the hilt of his sword shook Rynne from her perusal and she lifted her hands, palms out at chest height.

"No need for alarm, my lord. I will tell you all. But first..." A sudden remembrance of the vial had her reaching for her neck to feel for the chain and him pulling his sword.

He finished the sentence for her. "But first, I shall have that vial, lest you use it to cast a spell over my lands and the people I love, Witch."

Witch?

Rynne's mouth fell open. She'd been called a lot of things in her life, having grown up the youngest sibling behind two brothers, but to be hailed as a witch… Irritation outweighed any fear she felt and she bristled, sure that her nostrils must be flaring as she attempted to pull herself to her full height.

Of course, it wasn't like she hadn't just appeared out of nowhere, dressed in the peculiar clothing Corvona Bruxa had given her… but if he thought she would give up the vial, or more importantly, what was inside… it would be over her dead body.

She looked at the blade pointed in her direction as the man came closer and her heart sank. There was no way he was ever going to believe her. She dropped her chin to her chest and sighed. She still had try. The truth was all she had.

"I'm no witch," she said softly. "But the vial does contain a potion from one… at least I think it does."

She gulped as the tip of his sword wavered. Staring into his eyes, she prayed he would at least let her tell her story before he ran her through.

A huff of relief left her when he lowered his sword, even though he kept it at the ready. She flinched when he reached out his hand and pushed the material of her gown away from her neck. She held her breath, expecting him to grab hold of the chain. Instead, he traced his finger across her shoulder, making her shudder, especially when his eyes met hers.

"Explain this, then."

Rynne shivered at the low timbre of his voice. Dragging her gaze from his, she craned her neck so that she could see what he was talking about. Her eyes grew wide as she reached up to touch the darkened mark on her skin.

Blinking away the tears that threatened, she pressed her lips together for a moment, trying to steady their quivering.

"I... don't know, my lord. I can only tell you that m... my name is Rynne Willowthorne. It will make me sound daft, but I swear it is true... I fe... fell through time in an attempt to gain help for my brother's ailment. I don't know why I am in your garden or how this mark came to be upon me, but the vial is my only hope for helping him and I refuse to give it up." Rynne placed her hand over the vial beneath her dress. She closed her eyes, her lips moving in a silent prayer.

A small swish through the air had her cringing as she waited for the sting of his blade. Instead, she heard the sword slide into the leather of its sheath. Opening one eye and then the other, she found him squinting at her.

"Willowthorne?" he asked.

Rynne nodded.

He frowned. "And your brother's name?"

Her forehead creased with her lifted brows and she blinked a few times, confusion mixing with relief.

"K... Kensey, my lord. My brother is Kensey Willowthorne, Lord of Honorcrest in Wolfdenreve."

She bobbed a curtsey, confused at the smile he quickly hid.

"And what ails your brother, my lady?"

Rynne gritted her teeth, growing weary of the questions and yet knowing he held her future in his hands. She glanced at the sword in the scabbard at his side and shook her head.

"I don't know, my lord. Only that he has been unwell ever since he…" She stopped, biting at her lower lip until he commanded her to continue.

"He put on a ring and soon after collapsed to the floor. We've been unable to wake him since, so in a fit of desperation, I went to the old witch and she told me…"

"Mordrin," he cursed under his breath and Rynne nodded.

"Yes, Mordrin. She told me to collect the waters from the pool in the Cave of Dracha. When I tried, I fell in."

Rynne left out the part about feeling as though she'd been pushed. She finished her story to the point where she tossed her coin into the fountain, wishing to return home, and ended up surfacing in his pond. She stared at him, willing him to believe her while she watched the muscle in his jaw work as he thought.

"I know Willowthorne. I know what you say of his ailment is true…"

"Then you will help me?"

Forgetting herself, she stepped forward, placing her palms against his chest. Her eyes widened at the current that passed between them and she would have stepped away had his hands not closed over hers. She watched him fight to swallow, marveling at the heat that burst within her. When a light shudder shook her body, his arms went around her, pulling her closer.

"You're the missing sister... the Lady Katrynne," he whispered, his face so close to hers she could feel the heat of his skin.

Rynne nodded at his statement, and when his gaze slid to her lips, she couldn't help but wet them and he groaned.

Not quite sure how, her hands found the hair at the nape of his neck just as his mouth crashed down on hers, his tongue following the trail hers had taken only seconds before. Rynne's lips opened and she gasped when his tongue slid across her own, her tongue sparring back, stroking against his until they were both breathless. His eyes were huge when he finally pulled away.

"Do you believe in destiny, Katrynne Willowthorne? Because I believe Fate brought you to my home instead of yours."

His breath whispering across her cheek told her to say yes. Her heart beating against his and the pull of her body to press even closer to his screamed of the truth of his words. He felt so right. She wanted to say yes.

Instead, she pushed away and raised her hand to slap him. Only he was too fast, catching her wrist before she connected.

He stared down at her, disappointment evident in his glare. "I probably would have deserved that had you not been a willing party to that moment of folly." Lips that had teased hers, igniting a passion deep in her belly just seconds before, thinned.

Tears sprung to Rynne's eyes and she averted her gaze.

"Please," she whispered. "I just need to get home."

Chapter 4

Brendan stared at the woman before him wondering what had just happened. His senses had run amok, with words like Fate and Destiny swirling around in his head. Her story was utterly unbelievable. And yet, he believed her, especially with the mark that matched his in every way except color and its placement on the opposite shoulder. He still had no idea what was happening, but it appeared the Lady Katrynne had gone through time to collect what she believed was a cure for her brother.

He thought of the vial that had been visible under her wet clothing and had to fight to pull his thoughts from the vision of her breasts beneath the cloth. As odd as it was, he had the feeling the Raven Witch had meant to secure his desire for the woman in the clothes she chose for her, and she'd done a damned good job.

Clearing his throat, Brendan tried to shake the thoughts from his head.

"Your family will be most pleased to see you, though I doubt my men will be thrilled when I tell them we must ride again so soon after our return. The unrest in Thurwickden has made the trip quite tedious and we'll have to ride through it to get you home."

"Thurwickden?" She stiffened and he could almost see her lining up the facts. "Then you must be

Lord over the fief of Karthmere."

Brendan nodded. "Yes, my lady. I am Lord MacCailín of Locktonhurst."

Propriety demanded that he bow, and she curtsied, rising upon his command. He'd much rather have ordered her to kiss him again. Instead, he took her elbow and began to escort her toward his castle, hating the way his lips ached to taste her, the betrayal of his body in its desire to press her against him. He worked to control his breathing, hopeful she'd taken no notice of the way he was affected by her. He searched for a distraction.

"You know nothing more about the ailment that plagues Lord Willowthorne?"

Brendan noticed how the sunlight played off Lady Katrynne's coppery curls when she shook her head. He would have loved to stroke the silken threads, letting them slide through his fingers. He fought his concentration back to listen to her words.

"Kensey was fine, tending to his business as castle lord and being annoying like all brothers. Then, he fell ill, growing completely still." She cleared her throat and continued. "Several men visited our home, Honorcrest, just before. When we asked if they were men of the King, Kensey wouldn't say, only that he alone had business with them and that we should have nothing to do with them. It was shortly thereafter that he put on the ring and collapsed. The only thing that seemed odd at that point was that the ring refused to budge from his finger."

Brendan stopped abruptly and tried to look away, but Rynne turned, her eyes narrowing and locking with his.

"You know of the ring, don't you?"

Wrestling with his answer, Brendan nodded. He hadn't want to lie, but he didn't want to divulge all to her either.

"I saw it on his finger when I was there last, yes."

Her brows shot up.

"That's where you and your men were, then?"

He nodded, and she continued, her words tentative.

"My brother... he is well?"

Brendan started to nod again, then stopped himself. Her brother remained abed, unmoving, though the nourishment their mother managed to get down him had kept him alive. He told her as much.

"Do you believe there is hope for him?"

Brendan paused for a few seconds then confirmed that he did with a bob of his head.

"There's always hope... as long as someone believes," he stated, patting her arm.

He began walking, and from the corner of his eye, he could see her contemplating him. Her lips turned up in a tentative smile before her gaze went back to his castle.

"Thank you for that, my lord."

Brendan chuckled lightly, then frowned. His free hand fell to the pouch at his waist covering the oddly shaped lump among his other possessions. Would the men come to conduct *business* with him next?

At twenty and nine, he felt the weight of the world on his shoulders. He knew what the men had wanted from his friend, and when Kensey had placed the ring on his finger to keep them from getting it, something had gone awry. He knew why. It had been too early. His father had warned him that could happen if he had not yet reached the age of readiness.

But, if the men came, he knew he'd do the same thing Kensey had. As long as his friend remained alive, they couldn't take the ring. He glanced at the woman at his side and offered up a silent prayer that her belief in the potion was enough to assure her brother's life. Her belief was all they had, and if he was correct in his assumptions, it had already brought her home.

Rynne's senses reeled as she walked in silence beside the man who claimed to be Lord of Locktonhurst. She rolled her eyes. Of all the places Fate could have had her surface, it would have to be the lily pond of a man with deep blue eyes and lips that could set her afire with the slightest twitch. Feeling them on her own hadn't been bad either. She caught herself just before she sighed knowing she'd have to watch herself around him. She could already feel the tug on her heart.

Was that what Corvona Bruxa had meant with her parting words to be wary of the man who would attempt to steal her heart? She'd thought the witch had meant the vial that held the precious potion for her brother because of its shape, especially since there had already been several men after her that wanted it. She wasn't sure. Nothing seemed straightforward or clear. Perhaps now that she was home, or nearly so, life would begin to make sense again.

Rynne frowned when she looked up to see a dragon etched into the stone above the door they were approaching. Her body stiffened. How could anyone not detest the mythical creatures? Wrought with the same disgruntled rumblings from deep inside her that she always felt when she thought of dragons, Rynne looked away from the beast.

Dragons!

Her mother told her that at her birth, Shama—the old midwife and supposed Seer—had asserted that Rynne's spirit animal was a dragon. As a child, she'd dreamed one of the fabled beasts would visit her, and then later she'd watched for signs of scales to appear on her flesh, had spread her arms in hopes of sprouting wings that had never came. Age and cynicism had driven from her the ludicrous idea that they lived at all, or that she would somehow find the power within herself to morph into one of them.

The fact that the ring on her brother's hand had also been in the shape of a dragon caused her heart to plummet into the pit of her stomach. They were cursed, dragons were. She was sure of it. That was why she'd been unable to successfully remove the ring. There was power in the ring, and that power was somehow controlling her brother. The faster she got the potion to him, the sooner she could rid them all of the hideous thing.

"How soon do we begin this journey?" she asked, surprised by her own fervor.

"At first light," he answered without hesitation. "I'd leave now if we had more daylight ahead of us. We'll want to set up camp our first night within the far border of Karthmere so we can ride hard the next day in an attempt to get across the fiefdom of Thurwickden in one day."

Rynne nodded. "May I know the essence of the unrest within Lord Brantley's borders? It seems to have risen up so quickly, especially for a man so beloved by his serfs and servants alike."

When he raised his brows, she hurried on.

"His sister, Lady Isobella, has come to stay with us on occasion. I believe she may have a soft spot for my brother."

Rynne looked down, biting at her lip. She didn't know why she'd said that, especially knowing men cared little for ladies gossiping. She sighed. It didn't really matter. She'd be home in a couple of days, and given the distance, she'd probably never see this lord again. The thought left a hollow in the pit of her stomach.

Brendan's brows drew down and he averted his gaze to the ground. Could she truly not know how long she had been gone? The unrest had been ongoing, off and on, for several months, at least for the duration of her absence. He shook his head, wondering how much he should tell her.

Just older than himself and Kensey, Tamas Brantley, Lord of Garway, had inherited his fiefdom around the same time as the other two, their fathers all expiring during the lengthy battle of Volante. Brendan didn't want to think of that time any more than he wanted to acknowledge the wave of jealousy that hit him when he wondered if the maiden had already met Tamas and taken a fancy to him. She wouldn't have been the first.

A likable character, his dark-haired neighbor had a quick wit and an even faster tongue. Lord Brantley was said to have a way with the ladies. It was rumored that he'd sweet-talked one of the King's daughters into sharing her bed. Brendan wasn't sure just how much of that he believed, since the man still had his head and there'd been not even a hint of threatened nuptials. He had seemed to keep mostly to his own land since then.

The Lady Katrynne was correct in her assessment of his character. Those who served under him, whether that be on his lands or during their time at battle, all thought highly of him. He was the kind of man who would lay down his life for another should he deem that person worth his loyalty. Though if you were found to be his enemy...

Brendan shuddered, covering it with a shrug. He'd hold his tongue for now. There was no reason as yet to share with the maiden all that he knew, that the same men who had visited her brother had also foisted themselves into Brantley's castle and the Lord of Thurwickden had placed several of them in his dungeon. The ongoing battle was the usurper's attempt at gaining freedom for the other members of their league. Driagaran against Druajen… the bad against the good, just as it had always been.

Chapter 5

Brendan nodded at a guard who scrunched his brow in confusion as he and Rynne walked into the house. He almost laughed, realizing he'd have to find a way to explain her presence within his halls. Then again, he was lord there, accountable to no one except the King. How she got there was no one's concern and if he deemed the return of the lady to her family worthy of another ride through Thurwickden, so be it. They may not like it, but none of his men would challenge him. Being lord was a good position to be in. He smiled, turning his attention to watching the maiden take in his home for the first time.

No finer than her own, really, there were features that he knew were unique and truly breathtaking. His forefathers had been more blatant about who they were; their obsession with dragons becoming the central theme of the Keep.

The torchieres, spaced unevenly along the hall they walked down, were carved towers with stone dragons climbing up their walls. The main foyer sported a chandelier in the shape of a flying dragon hung high in the multi-story space. He couldn't wait for her to see the sculpture that stretched across the top of the fireplace in the dining hall, or those crawling up the posts of his bed.

No, no, no. *That* was probably one thing he should *not* consider showing her. Not that he would have minded. Their walk from the garden had done little to quench the fire from the kiss they'd shared. He thought of her reaction. Even with all the uncertainty and fear that she'd unsuccessfully tried to mask in her eyes, she had met his kiss with fervor, returning it with a passion few women would have shared, especially not with a man she'd just met.

There was something odd about her—about *them*. There was a feeling of intimacy between them—a knowing of one another. With the way she had kissed him back, he knew she'd felt it too, even if neither of them could have explained it.

Brendan took the opportunity to scrutinize her further when she looked up at the dragon chandelier until, after turning slowly, she lost her balance and stumbled back into him. Startled, her arms went out and he caught her, his hands on her forearms pulling her firmly against his chest.

"Don't worry," he whispered low against her ear, "I won't let you fall."

The gulp of air, slow blink, and the way she leaned into him for a moment before her wits returned and she stepped away, were worth more than the whole of his kingdom. He felt a stirring inside him. His dragon approved. Their alliance would be good, serving them, their families, and their kind.

When she cleared her throat, Brendan did the same before calling for Hilde. He frowned, surprised his sisters hadn't shown yet.

Distracted from his thoughts, he smiled at the appearance of the plump form of a maid who had been with his family for longer than he could remember. He waved off her curtsy and introduced her to the Lady Katrynne, feeling a fleeting pang of jealousy when the lady asked the old maid to call her Rynne. He wasn't surprised the lady had so quickly taken to the grandmotherly maid. Everyone did. Without her and Durstan, he would have been completely lost after his father's death, and even more so when his mother followed shortly thereafter.

"Hilde," he called after them. "Use the White Room for our guest, please."

He could see the concern on the lady's face after Hilde opened and closed her mouth several times, stammering out the beginning of sentences, only to stop. In the end, a raised brow had the maid lowering her head in obedience.

"You may use any of the belongings in the room. See that she wants for nothing."

Brendan skedaddled out of there before either of them could say anything more. He really did need to find Conall. His second in command would need the time between now and bedtime to prepare the men for their journey.

Whistling, he stopped by the kitchens first, ignoring the wide-eyed stares he received when he ordered a tray taken up to the White Room. Let them stare and whisper. She needed sustenance. He chuckled. Her stomach had grumbled most unladylike on the walk from the garden. She'd looked adorable cutting her eyes in his direction each time to see if he'd heard.

Wondering whether the unsteady feeling in her stomach was from hunger, being overwhelmed by her venture, or from the ravenous way Lord MacCailín had looked at her as they climbed the stairs, Rynne had to force herself to breathe normally while the maid fussed over her.

She couldn't get their kiss out of her head, nor the way her skin heated every time he touched her, no matter how lightly... Traveling through time seemed to have awakened a craving deep within her. She felt so reckless. How wantonly she had returned his kiss. No wonder he had smiled at her the way he did before taking his leave.

Rynne looked around the room—the room she knew without a doubt belonged to the Lady of the House. Its finery told her as much. There was also the door... Midway along one wall hung a reminder that this room was connected to another, to that of the Lord of the Castle. It was quite nearly an exact replica of the chambers her parents had shared. The door locked but one way, assuring the Lady could only pass into the Master's chamber when bidden, whereas the Lord could enter her room any time he wished.

Moisture clouded her vision. Why had Lord MacCailín placed her here? What expectations did he have for her, and would her willingness determine his inclination to help her get home?

Rynne jumped when a knock came on the hallway door and Hilde chuckled. Her hands full of odds and ends she was pulling from the wardrobe, she asked Rynne to answer it. No more surprises, she thought when she pulled it open, only to smile when she saw the food-strewn tray the servant carried. She motioned him inside, her stomach thanking him with a loud growl that wrung giggles from the two girls who came in behind him.

Rynne cocked her head as she turned toward them. One looked very much like a female version of the Lord of Locktonhurst. The other, a more petite blonde with wary blue eyes, regarded her with caution, her laughter fading away much faster than her sister's. They were sisters, she was sure, even without being told.

"We're Brendan's sisters," the darker haired one told her. "I'm Margaret, and this…" she turned to point at the younger of the two, "She's Sophia. We're told you're staying the night."

When Rynne nodded, Margaret clapped her hands. The girl may have been close to her own age, but she acted much younger.

"We don't get many lady visitors up here," Hilde provided. "I'm afraid their manners are a bit rusty, my lady. I… uh, the majority of their upbringin' has fallen to me, and... well, I'm no lady." The maid fixed the two girls with a steely glare when they snickered, her eyes softening as she continued. "Their mama, God rest her soul." The three crossed themselves and Rynne quickly did the same. "Well, you see, she didn't take to the loneliness up here so much and spent a good deal of her time at the King's Palace. Her time of confinement here during Volante nearly drove her bonkers..."

"I would have been going with her in another two years," Margaret interrupted.

Two years, Rynne thought. That would have put her at nineteen. They weren't that far off in age. She turned to look at the other girl who had yet to move further into the room.

"And what of you, Sophia? How long until you might go to the palace?"

The younger girl shocked her with the vehemence of her shaking head, her gaze going to the floor when Hilde chastised her. It was Lady Margaret who solved the riddle.

"Five years, but she can't go now because we have no one to take us since Mama..." she crossed herself again and cleared her throat before continuing. "Sophia has no interest in life outside of Locktonhurst anyway. She may look like our mother, but she's MacCailín through and through. She'd rather explore this old rock or gaze out at the sea than don a frilly dress and dance with a prince."

The way Margaret clasped her hands together, her

face lighting up as she said the last, told Rynne that was exactly what *she* wanted to do. What girl wouldn't want to give up the solitariness of life in a castle so far from Court to find the man of her dreams?

Rynne looked at Sophia and then out the window. She could see the vast expanse of water in the distance, imagined the sound of it hitting the shore somewhere beneath them and thought the exploration of both the castle and the grounds would be a welcomed excursion.

An invitation to the Palace had arrived for her that year and she'd turned it down. The thought of venturing beyond the borders of Wolfdenreve terrified her. She had no desire to dance with strange men or wear frilly dresses for more than just the occasional festival held within the great hall of her own home…

Lady Margaret's voice startled her and she realized the girl had been talking the whole time she'd been lost in thought. Hilde must think her manners as deplorable as her charges. Not so. Her parents may have practically hidden her away from visitors to Honorcrest, but she'd still been schooled in both books and conduct, and the decision to refrain from going to the Palace had been wholly hers.

"Brendan could take us," Margaret was saying. "But he won't. He scarcely stays put here, and yet, he detests the affairs of the Palace." She squinted at Rynne who squinted back. "If you're thinking you'll win his favor as a way to get into the Royal Circle, you may as well think again. You won't be the first to have tried." She stood from the chair where she'd plopped down and walked toward the door. "There's only one thing he's interested in, and it's sure not a trip to the courts… or the altar."

Rynne glanced at Hilde as the girl slipped from the room. The maid's mouth hung as wide open as her own. What a tart little snip, she thought. Lady Margaret needed to be bent over someone's knee.

She lifted her chin and turned toward the other sister, wondering if she'd encounter more of the same. Sophia stood rooted to the spot where she'd been since the two had entered the room. Rynne studied her as the girl drew herself up, her shoulders going back in an attempt to match her pose.

"Do you intend to try to marry Brendan?" she asked, her voice low and soft.

Sucking in a shallow breath, Rynne started to answer and then shrugged. Did she?

"I've only just met your brother."

The blonde head bobbed as Sophia turned toward the door. She too, stopped at the threshold.

"Do… do you know the meaning of the black feathers?" she asked.

Her odd question knocked Rynne completely off guard. She shook her head after staring at the girl for a few seconds too long and rubbed her shoulder as she turned away. She could feel Sophia's gaze boring into her before the door closed with a soft thud. She looked at Hilde, who watched her closely as she might someone she was looking out for.

Biting at her lip, Rynne began to remove the tabard, pulling the neckline of her gown to the side when she was finished. She walked toward the portly maid.

"Have you any idea what this is and why it has appeared?"

"Don't be afraid," Hilde told her. "You'll know soon enough."

Chapter 6

The meal was as good as any that had been served at Honorcrest, yet Rynne found herself unable to eat much of it. Nerves and fatigue knitted themselves together in a growing ball in her stomach. Hilde had done her best to put her at ease while she helped her bathe and dress for dinner, but the blatant absence of both Margaret and Sophia at the table had her wondering if the maid had also informed Brendan of the happenings in the room she now occupied.

Thinking of Locktonhurst's lord as Brendan, sleeping in the Lady's Chamber... it was all too familiar, too... intimate.

Attempting to distract herself, she spoke to the Lord seated across from her position in the place of honor at Brendan's right hand.

"Where had you been?" she asked Conall, Brendan's second in command.

A handsome man in his own right with an ever-ready smile, his large frame shook when he laughed.

"Out looking for you, my lady."

Rynne gasped, her fingers fluttering to her chest.

"Me? That... that seems a bit extreme."

"Considering you were gone almost five score days, my lady, there are those who might beg to differ..."

Her body tensing, Rynne seemed unable to control the rising pitch of her voice.

"Five score? Over three months?"

How could that be when it had been less than a day for her? She felt suddenly dizzy, wishing she could find a way to be alone to sort out the thoughts swirling in her head.

"Aye, Lady. 'Tis why our lord has commanded that we leave on the morrow, making haste to return ye to yer family," one of the knights from further down the table offered.

All eyes turned toward Hilde, who sat even further down.

"What? With all due respect, Master Brendan, surely you can't be serious."

Leaning back in his seat, Brendan raised a lazy brow.

"What beef have you with this plan, Hilde? Were it one of your girls, you'd be hollering for their quick return, no?"

Hilde frowned at him. "Well, yes, Master, but… a Lady, with you and all your men. Alone? Seems…"

"Ah," he interrupted. "And who do you propose I take? One of my sisters?" He shook his head. "I've made up my mind. My reputation will be enough to secure the Lady's good character."

There were a couple of snickers from down the table and another of his guard—a man named Johanasin—dared to speak.

"Especially with the lady already sharing the

Master's chambers," he said behind his hand.

The silence in the hall was broken only by the thrumming of Brendan's fingers against the table. After a few seconds, he cleared his throat.

"I hope you will enjoy your days of rest, Martin," he addressed a young man toward the end of the table. "Sir Johanasin will be glad to take over your duties of mucking the stables this next week." He smiled at the gasps from around his table.

A knight cleaning dung from the barn? When the knight and the stable hand both nodded, she realized there would be no one who dared oppose his orders. He was, indeed, Lord of Locktonhurst. She was both concerned and awed.

"Eat," he whispered quietly, leaning toward her. "You'll need your strength."

The meal couldn't have ended quickly enough for Rynne. She was shaking by the time they reached the door to the room she would occupy during her night at Locktonhurst. Lord MacCailín had commented on her state several times, asserting that she must be exhausted from her ventures.

Rynne confirmed that she was, hopeful it would stop any untoward thoughts he might have, but when he entered the chamber instead of simply depositing her at the threshold, she thought she might lose the scant food she had managed to eat.

Brendan frowned when he looked at her and when he placed his palm against her forehead, he laughed at the way she jumped.

"It appears you run no fever, at least," he stated, taking her chin in his hand.

He tipped her head this way and that, squinted, nodding after a moment, then leaned toward her. "You're quite safe within my walls, my lady. I assure you."

His voice, so low and close, reverberated through her and she shivered, even though she wasn't cold. She could see the fire in his eyes and she closed her own, waiting for the kiss that would begin her undoing.

With a pat on her arm, Lord MacCailín walked away from her and she wheeled around, watching to see what he was doing. Contemplating the room, he finally grabbed the chair from the small writing desk and walked back to place it against the connecting door, jamming it beneath the knob securing that no one would enter the chamber without someone on the inside releasing it.

Rynne narrowed her eyes, trying to anticipate his next move.

With a slow chuckle, he crossed to the door that would lead him into the hallway and removed a key hanging on the wall beside the jam. He held it up, then opened the door before slipping the key into the lock on the inside.

"Hilde will be here shortly to assure that you have everything, though most of what you need for a good night's rest has already been laid out for you, my lady. I suggest you do your best to use the hours of darkness wisely for it is bound to be the most restful night you'll have for the next two days."

Brendan bowed and wished her goodnight before vanishing behind the closed doors.

Rynne's feet seemed rooted to the floor, her mouth threatening to remain in a perpetual state of openness until she managed to clamp it shut. Uttering a low growl, her nostrils flaring, she spun around and walked to the bed. She picked up a small pillow and threw it toward the door. Curse him! Curse *her*. Had she truly been about to hand him her virtue with little more than a sheer veil of weak fear?

She plopped down on the edge of the bed and plucked at a loose bead on the lap of her borrowed dress.

"What's happening to me?"

She looked up then back down as the first teardrop fell, oblivious of the black feather that lay near the chair that Lord MacCailín had used as a barrier between them. She knew he had blocked the door to ease her concerns and she should be thankful for his courtliness. Why then did she feel so bereft?

Brendan stood in the hallway just outside the door of the room that would one day belong to the lady of Locktonhurst. Walking away from the actual lady inside had been one of the hardest things he had ever done, especially knowing the two ladies were one and the same. Seducing her now would have been so easy. He knew her head was in a spin and that part of her wanted him every bit as much as he wanted her. He could feel the pull.

With heavy steps, he walked to his room. The discipline he'd garnered from his training as a knight was the only reason he'd be able to sleep, especially knowing a chair and his honor were the only things separating them.

Chapter 7

Brendan bolted upright. He heard the storm outside beating down on his castle, but that wasn't what awakened him. He listened until the noise came again—a quiet tap against the door that connected the room of the master of the house to that of his lady. He'd barely managed to slip into his britches when he heard the chair scratching against the floor and the door creaking open. It had been a long time since the seal had been broken and the hinges protested. He squinted against the darkness, his heart racing as an ethereal figure appeared.

"My lord."

His thoughts exactly. Tendrils of lightning shot through him every bit as strong as those beyond his windows.

"What do you need, my lady?" He swallowed loudly, his own need making the simple task difficult. He heard the unsteadiness in her voice when she spoke again from her position between the rooms.

"The r... rain has extinguished the fire and my candle has grown too short..." She paused overlong. "I'm sorry to have to say that I am in need of the chamber pot and... I cannot navigate an unknown place in the dark." She added the last when he didn't answer.

His eyes adjusted and he could see her biting at her bottom lip. He only hoped she couldn't see that he was fighting laughter. Then his brow crinkled. How in the world had the rain affected the room's fire?

He started toward the door then remembered the chamber pot. Moving to the hearth, he stooped down to light a tender from the low-burning fire, touching it to the two candles that sat on his mantle. When he crossed back to where she stood, he handed her one and pointed to the screen in the far corner of his own room.

"I'll see to the fire," he told her when he tried to brush past.

Rynne stepped back, her eyes narrowing, her mouth slightly open as if to speak even though she didn't.

"You'll find what you need there," he waved his hand again, "and you'll have your privacy while I'm in the other room."

She nodded and skirted past him on her tiptoes, obviously hoping to keep from touching him in the close proximity of the doorway. Brendan had to bite his own lip to keep from laughing again.

From his squatted position in front of the fireplace, Brendan looked over his shoulder when he heard the whisper of her slippered feet returning from his room. Brushing his hands together, he stood, enjoying how the multiple candles he'd lit washed her in their glow. He'd never considered the idea of copper hair to hold intrigue, but she had proved him wrong.

The thick plait that draped over her shoulder drew his attention to breasts that invited a cuddle. The tendrils that had sprung free begged him to push them behind her ear with petal soft caresses. The locks complimented her, completing her beauty instead of taking away from it.

Brendan smiled, noting that she maintained her distance.

"I trust you feel better."

She nodded her head and he chuckled.

"Unfortunately, there's no such easy answer to the extinguished fire. It appears birds have, at some point, found their way into the chimney and the rains have caused their nests to disintegrate, dumping waterlogged debris and feathers into the fireplace. It's too dangerous to send anyone up in this weather. It will have to wait until the storm stops."

Brendan watched as she took in the feathers and bits and pieces of mud and grass that had once been nests now strewn in front of the fireplace. He hoped she wouldn't become as anxious as his sisters thinking the black feathers were some sort of omen.

Instead, she uttered a quiet *oh* that allowed him a chance to direct her attention away from any telling foreshadow she might be conjuring up in her head.

"But… I did find additional tapers for you. Perhaps if you leave one burning behind the screen you'll be able to find your way…"

Even in the low light of the few candles he could

see her cheeks growing red. No doubt discussing bathroom needs with a man was not something she was accustomed to. He stifled a chuckle, surprised to see her offer a tentative smile.

"You are most kind, Lord MacCailín. Your superlative hospitality rivals your reputation."

Brendan raised a single brow. He supposed he shouldn't be surprised at her formality any more than he was her distance. She was, after all, a maiden alone in a bedroom with the lord of the keep.

"You have heard me well-spoken of, then? I suppose that is most ardently desirable to the contrary," he answered in light jest.

When he mocked her formality, attempting to put her at ease, they both laughed, hers ending in a shiver. Brendan frowned, especially when she closed her arms about herself.

"You're cold, my lady." He noted and was already pulling the shawl from the back of the chair near the fireplace. "Perhaps you should take my room. The fire is low, but it remains warm..."

His words trailed off as he wrapped the throw around her shoulders, sucking in a too loud breath when he looked down to find her lips slightly parted, her eyes boring into his.

"Especially with the lady already sharing the Master's quarters," she repeated the words Johanasin had spoken at their meal.

"Especially then," he whispered, lowering his mouth to hers.

With deliberate slowness, he brushed his lips across hers before pulling back.

"I'll not force myself upon you, my lady. I told you before, you have nothing to fear from me. I'll not do anything that you do not desire."

She shivered again. "Then I fear for my reputation upon the greeting of the morning light."

Chapter 8

Rynne fought through the dream that someone was beating down the gates with a battering ram. She woke to realize it was someone at the chamber door. Sitting too quickly, she winced at how sore she was and in places she wasn't used to being sore.

Squinting, she looked up, her mouth gaping at the sight of Lord MacCailín's bare backside as he jumped and shoved his legs into his britches. The memory of the night before flooded her mind, her body reacting at the thoughts of his hands, his mouth on her, their bodies entwined, uniting… She turned her head to the side, the red streak on the bedsheets rising up as a blatant indictment.

Dear Lord, what had she done? Her trip through time must have muddled her senses more than she'd thought. She looked up as he went toward the door, her eyes going wide. She wasn't addled enough to let someone see her so brazenly in his bed no matter what he had promised her. She also wasn't so naive to not know men promised ladies many things that evaporated with the darkness.

Rolling, Rynne slid to her feet with the bed sheet tangled around her and scurried across the floor, skirting through the connecting door and closing it just as she heard the plank scraping open in the Master's chamber. Her ear to the wood, she could hear the anxious rise of Hilde's voice. Though she couldn't catch every word, she heard enough to know the maid had stopped by her room first and was concerned that she hadn't answered her knocking.

Rynne looked around. She could feign that she'd been in a heavy sleep, but her nightdress was nowhere to be found. She scrambled to remember at what point it had been discarded, feeling quite wicked at the tingling between her legs that the memory produced. Never in a million years would she ever have imagined that the happenings between a man and woman could feel the way the Lord of Locktonhurst had made her feel.

She ran a hand across her breast, naked beneath the sheet. His mouth upon her there had been a slice of heaven and hell rolled into one with the way he'd made her ache, begging for release with little more than his tongue and teeth. And when he'd rained kisses down her belly... even now, the thought made her breath come more quickly.

Rynne closed her eyes, the vision of him smiling up at her just before he touched his tongue to her sex would forever be imprinted in her mind, as would that moment when he'd pressed himself into her, joining them together as one for the first time. They'd repeated the act twice before sleep pulled her into its depths... until the knocking on the door had wakened them.

She shook her head, realizing the knocking was no longer in her memory. She could hear Hilde telling

Brendan to try again, which he did, calling her name this time.

She started for the door then remembered her nightdress and changed directions. When the hinges creaked on the connecting door, she winced but continued her mission, quickly discarding the sheet on his bed and pulling the gown over her head. With silent steps, she returned to her room.

"Coming!" she yelled, just as another round of pounding ceased at the door to the hallway. "My goodness!" She fanned her face as she opened the door.

"Oh, thank heavens." Hilde crossed herself, pushing past Brendan and wrapping plump arms around her. "You gave this old heart of mine quite a fright. Are you well?" She stepped back, turning Rynne in a circle as she looked her over.

Rynne gave a little laugh, her eyes finding those of Lord MacCailín. "Yes. Quite well, actually. Just tired and… well, I had need of dealing with delicate matters."

"Of course, dear." Turning toward Brendan, Hilde shooed him away with the waving of her hands before linking her arm in Rynne's and leading her toward the wardrobe. "Master Brendan has afforded you full access to these fine garments, my lady, though if you will allow, I believe I know the perfect gown for your trip."

Rynne bobbed her head toward the older woman. "I would be honored and truly appreciative of your assistance, Hilde. In fact, if I could, I would take you home with me."

They laughed and Hilde gave her a bit of a side hug

while looking over her shoulder and winking at Brendan. When she turned back, Rynne dared a peek at the door. Brendan inclined his head in her direction before turning away. It was filled with enough warmth to cause her cheeks to flame as she listened to him humming—a sound that continued beyond the door that connected his room to hers.

Light steps took Brendan back to his room. The bright smile Lady Katrynne had flashed at him caused another surge of arousal. He'd never imagined a night so magical as the one they'd just shared. Not that he was a stranger to the magic found when sheathed in a woman's warmth. But this had been different, so right in every way.

Walking to the bed, he ran his finger beside the crimson swatch on the linen before he began to fold it so that no one would find it and he might preserve her dignity on their wedding night. He breathed through another wave of raw desire. He'd imagined she'd be a passionate lover from the kiss they'd shared, and she hadn't disappointed. The thought of her soft skin pressed against him had his body growing harder still.

He turned, pulling the rope that would summon his squire. The sooner they left for Honorcrest, the better it would be for all of them.

Chapter 9

Rynne was surprised by the number of men assembled in the courtyard when Brendan escorted her out so that they could get on their way.

"Do you leave anyone to defend your castle?" she asked him quietly when he moved to assist her onto the palfrey that had been chosen for her.

Brendan chuckled. "There are men aplenty who will stay behind, though your safety is my main focus." He laughed again as he swung into the saddle of his destrier. "I assure you, I have no fear of anyone getting through my gates." Straightening his shoulders, he began to move, her horse falling in beside his and his men closing in around them, all without a word being spoken.

He smiled at her as they moved through the gate, awe causing her jaw to slacken when she realized why he had little worry. Locktonhurst had not only been built on the side of a sheer cliff that they had to wind their way down, but another wall had been erected below, complete with moat and guards. It would have taken a massive army to get into his fortress.

"My family has owned these lands for a long time. We've fought many battles and had more years to learn how best to protect what we hold dear."

Rynne nodded, swiveling in her saddle so that she

might take it all in. She noticed the Dragons on the portcullis as they passed under the arch and into the unprotected lands of Karthmere. She felt no fear though. This man, she sensed, would give his life to protect hers if he had to. And anyone wishing either of them ill would have to go through his men to get there. She found it hard to believe there were those out there who would be dumb enough to try.

The day passed without event, though Rynne had stayed close by Brendan's side. Even in those moments she'd needed to relieve herself, he'd insisted that her safety was more important than her privacy. He had, at least, preserved some of her dignity by turning his back and commanding his inner circle of men who were charged with her care to do the same, even as they encircled her at a respectable distance. Rynne had rolled her eyes at first, but as darkness began to overtake them, she was glad for his attentiveness. The scurrying of small animals sounded much larger and was more unsettling in the fading light.

When the low-burning fire they'd used to cook their meals was extinguished, nothing but the stars and moon to light the woodsy area where they had all begun to make their beds, Rynne felt true concern for the first time. She was bone tired and sore from riding for so long... not to mention the previous night's activities. All of that adding to the fact that she'd never spent the night without a roof over her head, set her emotions on edge.

Brendan had told her when they set out that it would be a much faster trip and they'd pass through with less detection if they stayed clear of all towns and abbeys. Wanting only to get home, she had agreed wholeheartedly without thought to where they would sleep or the inconveniences of traveling in a way the knights were accustomed to but no lady ever would be.

Now, she looked up at the sky growing steadily darker and felt a tear forming in the corner of her eye. She willed it away. Emotional outbursts weren't routine for her and she certainly didn't want any of these men to think her weak. Wishing for a soft pillow, she turned her face into the rolled blanket beneath her head so that no one would hear, only to feel a warm body sliding under the blanket that covered her.

"Fret not, my love."

Brendan's voice tickled the back of her ear, his breath warm as it fanned across her cheek.

Rynne wiped her palm against the corner of her eye and pressed her back into him, relishing the comfort of his arms going around her. She didn't care what anyone might say if they awakened. Having him near had calmed her instantly and she needed that, no matter the cost. She drifted to sleep, dreaming that he had called her his love.

Chapter 10

Shivering, Rynne wakened just before the sun began to peak above the horizon. She rolled to see Brendan nestled into his own bed sack a scant two feet from her, exactly where he'd been when they'd first bedded down for the night.

The indentation beside her was still warm, making her smile. He'd been most gentlemanly throughout the hours he'd been beside her. She'd been surprised, especially considering that she had awakened a few times to feel the evidence of his desire pressed against her backside.

It had been difficult for her as well having him so near. Exhaustion had warred with her own arousal— her need to feel him versus her need to sleep. The few snores from some of the other men close by had been the final bit of encouragement and she'd allowed sleep to pull her under each time, no longer afraid of whether she would wake upon the morn. Now, her body burned for him, making her regret her decision.

Brendan threw back his covers and jumped to his feet, turning to survey the camp and the men already beginning to make ready to leave. When his eyes lit upon her, she could see the same burning passion reflected back at her.

"Good morning, my lady." His gaze swept down

her, making her shiver. "I trust you slept well."

Rynne could see the slight lifting of the corners of his mouth and she had to bite her own lips to keep from returning the smile.

"Quite well. Thank you."

Tearing her gaze from his, Rynne attempted at a dignified rise, though her aching body protested, causing her to groan. She heard a chuckle from behind her and turned to see Lord Conall. He greeted her with a bow of his head and a bright smile.

"It takes some getting used to, these days in the saddle."

The wink to his lord that he thought she hadn't seen had her wondering whether he knew the full extent of why she was sore. She looked down and nodded.

"Unfortunately, I'm afraid today will be no better. We'll have to make haste to make up for the time we lost yesterday," he told her.

Rynne knew they'd had a slower start due to the heavy downpour causing mudslides and several of the streams they'd crossed to swell, forcing them to go further to find a safer way to cross over. Their pace had been relentless after that. She couldn't imagine going any faster.

She sighed and several more of the men joined in the chuckling. Head raising, Rynne squared her shoulders, determined to prove that she could withstand whatever came her way.

"Let us make ready then. I should hate to be the

cause of any further delay."

In the span of two hours, the group crossed the border into Thurwickden, a thin strip of water separating the two fiefdoms. To her left, Conall lifted his hand in the air, his fingers rising in some unknown configuration before he made a sweeping motion first one way and then another. Two groups of men broke off from the rest, each riding ahead in different directions.

Her brows down, Rynne looked at Brendan who merely put a finger to his mouth. She nodded, her senses tingling. Did they suspect something or was this routine when entering the lands of another? She knew the unrest Thurwickden had been experiencing would have them all more cautious as well, but she hadn't expected it so quickly after their crossing.

When another three hours passed without incident, the sun climbing into position above them reminding her that sustenance was a mandatory inconvenience, she'd begun to believe the extreme carefulness had all been for naught. Her bum hurt from the constant jostle of the fast-moving horses and her hands hurt from gripping the saddle horn, not to mention she had need of the make-shift privy. A sideways glance at Lord MacCailín told her he was aware of her distress.

"There's a small clearing with a pond not too far ahead. We'll stop there to rest and eat," he told her.

Rynne nodded and thanked him in the same quiet tones he'd used. It wasn't as if talking would have been any louder than the movement of so many horses, but silence seemed to be the order of the day.

"The other men have not returned. Do you not fear for their safety?" she asked Brendan as they chatted quietly over their meal. She'd noticed throughout the day that more small groups had been commanded to head off or fall back.

Brendan shook his head. "I'd be more concerned if they had." When she frowned, he leaned closer. "Much like your privy breaks, they've spread out to encircle us. It would take someone rising from our midst to penetrate the fortress we've created to protect you."

Rynne stilled, breathing only by sheer will, her gaze dropping to his lips so very close to her. If she moved her head just slightly forward... Brendan chuckled and backed away. Her cheeks heating, she closed her eyes. Good heavens, this man addled her senses.

Rising, she made her way to the pool and knelt. The cool water on her face would feel good. As she cupped her hands and reached to fill them, a ripple slid across the clear surface, an image of the fountain with the dragon materializing before her. Rynne screamed and thrust herself backwards, landing on her rear and finding four men instantly at her sides, their swords drawn. Brendan raced forward, his eyes wide, surveying the area as he finished tying the drawstring of his britches, his tunic falling back into place.

"What is the danger, my lady?" he asked, holding out his hand to her.

Rynne grasped his fingers, allowing him to pull her up, her rounded eyes contrasting the shaking of her head.

"I… I'm sorry. It m… must have been just a shadow.

Brendan stared at her for a moment before slowly nodding his head and dismissing his men with a slight wave of his hand.

When the others had moved to a respectable distance, he grabbed her arm, pulling her closer.

"What did you really see?" he asked, his voice low, firm.

Rynne's hesitation, she knew, spoke volumes.

"An image," she whispered, her hand moving to lay lightly against her chest. "The men… at the fountain…" She'd told him of her ventures as she'd laid in his arms during that first night so she knew he knew what she was talking about, even with her few words.

"Rynne." His eyes locked with hers and he continued to speak quietly. "I need to tell you something. Those men… I fear they are Driagaran."

When she covered her mouth with her free hand, he pulled her closer, his arms encircling her. She laid her head against his chest, his palm brushed against her cheek, and he pressed a quick kiss to the top of her hair.

Driagaran. That wasn't possible. Men who morphed into dragons were just a myth... The image she'd seen in the pool filled her mind, the men becoming clearer. They'd been wearing rings similar to the one she couldn't get off her brother's hand. Still, it couldn't be. The Driagaran were considered evil in the fables. Kensey couldn't be one of them.

Almost as if he could read her mind, Brendan spoke.

"There are two kinds of shifters. Rynne, listen to me."

When she started to shake her head, he took her chin in his hand, forcing her to look at him.

"The Druajen are from a different lineage. They are men who are dragons that have pledged their allegiance to our King and his lands. Your brother..."

Pulling in an unsteady breath, Rynne interrupted with her own conclusions.

"And Brantley. That's the reason for the unrest in his land." She closed her eyes then opened them wide. "And... you." Her eyes grew damp as she stared at him like he was some sort of monster.

"And me." He held her arm when she tried to pull back. "The mark on your shoulder, I think it means..."

Rynne screamed when dragons shot from the pool at Brendan's back. She heard him curse as he pushed her away, telling her to run to the trees. A split second of frozen uncertainty had him yelling at her again and she finally ran, the scrape of his sword sliding from the scabbard urging her forward.

At the edge of the forest she turned, slinking down behind a large tree. Eyes wide, Rynne tried to take in the battle before her. She counted as best as she could. There were at least seven dragons in the clearing, their massive bodies filling the space. Two took to the air on wings that looked too sheer to support them and she noticed there were more above them in the skies. She couldn't see Brendan, had no idea if he was man or beast. Her view became more obscured by the dirt and debris stirred up by the battle. It was hard trying to figure out who was friend and who was foe.

The bodies of several men and two of the dragons fell to the ground near Rynne. She heard a hideous scream, the ground shaking as another collapsed close to her hiding place. She whimpered when she saw the hilt of the sword that was buried in the spot where it's neck connected to its body.

The Locktonhurst crest was clearly visible on the pommel, Brendan's signifying stone shining from the middle. She closed her eyes, offering up a prayer for the now unarmed man, provided he was still man. She surmised that since he was using his sword, he hadn't changed. Why? She thought back, unable to recall him wearing a ring like the others. If he had, she surely would have remembered.

As the remaining dragons took to the sky and the

dust cleared, she could see a handful of men still in hand to hand combat. She gagged, trying to hold in her lunch as the huge bodies of the dead beasts morphed back into man form. Her heart slammed against her chest, eyes wide and wild as she continued to search for Brendan before she finally spotted him. Three men surrounded him, attempting to get a hold of his arms. Only one had a sword, though he didn't seem to be trying to run Brendan through.

The water, she thought. They were slowly backing him toward the water.

Rynne stood, her legs protesting the crouched position she'd been in for too long. Raising her chin and her arms, she prayed for strength and guidance, breaking her gaze away from the scene before her only long enough to locate Brendan's sword. It had fallen to the ground when the dragon changed back into a man.

She didn't quiver when she picked up the heavy blade, didn't gag at the blood along its edges. She didn't even yell as she lifted it high above her head and ran across the clearing, swinging it, listening to the swooshing as it broke the air, separating the head of Brendan's armed attacker from his body. Stumbling, she caught her footing just in time to run another one through when he lunged for her, then turned to find Brendan rolling on the ground with the third one.

When Brendan's attacker managed to grab the hilt of a dead man's sword, Rynne did scream, the blood curdling sound stopping the fighting all around just long enough to give the Locktonhurst men the upper hand over the remaining Driagaran.

All except one.

Rynne watched in horror as the short blade pierced Brendan's side. In slow motion, he pushed the man away, twirling him in the process and twisting his arm to where the man would fall on the same blade that had left the hole in his side. Stumbling, Brendan moved toward her, going down after a couple of steps. Rynne screamed again, his sword falling to the ground beside her before she ran, dropping to her knees beside the gasping man.

"My lord," she cried, her eyes brimming with tears. Brendan watched her, his gaze heavy, slow smile evaporating in a grimace. He grabbed his side, a painful chuckle causing him to groan.

"You are safe," he managed to croak out.

Rynne glanced over her shoulders to see that only his men remained standing. She nodded, crouching over him when he fought to suppress another moan, his hand pressed to his side. Dear God, she thought, don't let him die.

The vial swung free as she leaned forward, reminding Rynne of her mission. What cruelty Fate had foisted on her. Had she not gone for the potion in the first place, this man would have had no need to shed his own blood to save her. He'd be home, safe within the walls of his castle and her heart would be none the wiser that she could love someone so completely in such a short amount of time.

He reached for her, his hand slapping the potion

bottle instead. Instinctively, Rynne grabbed it, the action jolting her, causing her to break the chain.

The potion bottle in one hand, his in her other, Rynne frowned. Since the potion was to restore her brother, would it also work to save Brendan? If she gave it to him, then she'd have none for her brother. Could she get more? What if it didn't work and she wasted it and neither lived?

So many questions tumbled through her head. She couldn't make this choice. Her heart raced and she closed her eyes. How could she choose?

How could she not?

Pulling the cork free from the vial, Rynne positioned the opening near his lips, willing her hands to stop trembling. It wouldn't do to lose any of the precious liquid. She tapped the last of the drops into his mouth and waited. Nothing happened.

"Please," she whispered. "Help him."

The Ring.

Eyes wide, Rynne looked over her shoulder to where the voice had come from. No one was there, and still she heard the words again.

"There is no ring!" she screamed.

When his breath stilled, she wailed, collapsing against his chest, her hand landing over the pouch at his waist. Precious seconds passed before she realized it held more than coin. She sat up, working her fingers into the pouch and pulling out the hard item. She gasped. It was a ring exactly like the one her brother wore.

With tears in her eyes, she crossed herself and slipped the ring onto his finger, nearly screaming when the bush closest to her began to shake. She scanned the area, noting the only sword within her reach was the one the other man had used on Brendan. She couldn't force herself to reach for it, not with his blood covering the blade. If whoever was coming through the brush was enemy and this was truly the end, at least she would die beside the man who had so swiftly managed to snare her heart. She lay her head on his chest, her tears mingling with the moisture that was already there. *Please*, she thought again, *don't let us die before I can tell him I love him.*

Conall and several of the other Locktonhurst men burst through the brush into the clearing just as the first convulsion tossed Brendan's body into the air, throwing Rynne back toward them. She watched in horror as Brendan's frame twisted, bowing his back, only his shoulders and his feet touching the ground. He looked toward them, eyes wide, unseeing, mouth contorted in a silent scream that had Rynne groaning and tugging against the man who held her back.

To her side, Conall yelled his name, telling him to relax, to let the transformation take place. Brendan shuddered, his body rolled, limbs flailing to some unheard melody. A deep, guttural growl sounded in his throat and he stood, his shoulders rounding, arms outstretched. From inside him, bones popped, tendons loosened and tightened. Rynne turned, burying her face in the chest of one of the guards, covering her ears with her hands. She couldn't bear it.

Brendan looked down to see his reshaped body covered in scales, though he was surprised to see them much less reptilian than he had imagined they would be. The first transformation, he'd been told, would be the most difficult. They hadn't been wrong. Having one's form snapped and pulled, molding into another being, was tougher than the others had made it look. Feather-like scales covered him. They were beautiful, the color of moonlit glass, and when he lifted his arms, wings had taken their place—wings that seemed a ghostly gossamer, yet they were strong... strong enough, he knew, to lift his massive body and carry it through the air.

But not now. Now he had to see to the lady. He'd heard her screams, seen her fighting, and... Willing his body to return to human form, Brendan transformed and picked up the empty vial. On shaky legs, he walked toward the group. His hands on her shoulders, he whispered her name.

Rynne tensed, her eyes huge as she turned around before throwing herself at him, her arms wrapping around his neck as she tried to hug the very breath from him.

Laughing, Brendan twirled her around, kissing her soundly when she released him enough so that he could see her face.

Still feeling the vial in his palm, he pulled back

and opened his hand. "You saved my life... but what of your brother?"

She smiled at him through her wet lashes.

"I had no guarantee it would work... for my brother or for you. But I couldn't watch you die knowing there might be a chance..." A strangled sob stopped her words. "I'll get more. I have to be able... you said yourself that I just have to believe."

"There's always hope as long as someone believes," Brendan nodded as he repeated the words he'd said to her in the garden.

A warmth filled his hand and he held the vial upright between his thumb and finger, watching in awe as the liquid replenished itself.

Unknown words whispered in the wind as a black feather floated to the ground.

"Corvona Bruxa," Rynne whispered, new tears joining the others on her already wet cheeks. "Thank you, my friend."

Without anyone asking them, Brendan's men fell to the ground to search for the stopper that would keep the life-giving potion inside the vial. Brendan pulled a pendant from the front of his tunic and slipped it from the chain. Rynne caught his wrist, studying the metal dragon for a few seconds before letting him drop it into his pouch. He handed her the chain, knowing she'd need it to secure the vial. Ah, how he'd love to be that vial when it was nestled between her breasts...

He shuddered. This was not the time to let

renewed lust settle in. They needed to get on their way to Honorcrest. They'd defeated the dark forces of the Driagaran this time, but there would be more. There were always more. That's how it had been throughout the ages, the evil Driagaran shifters trying to get the protective force—the Druajen shifters to join them or risk death, their goal being to extinguish his kind so that they could take over the whole kingdom.

Brendan wasn't going to let that happen, especially now that Fate had sent a she dragon as his mate. Even now, the future of the Druajen could be growing in her womb. The thought made him nearly giddy, threatening to overwhelm him. He'd noticed his senses being much sharper since his transformation. He could live with that, though for now, he needed to focus on getting them to her family home of Honorcrest.

Helping Rynne replace the stopper and threading his chain through the eyelet, he watched her slip the vial over her head. With a smile, he took her arm to guide her back toward their waiting horses, a thought hitting him as they approached.

"How old are you, my lady?"

He knew it was an odd question to be asking at that time, and he almost laughed when she hesitated to answer. She finally shrugged.

"Twenty and one. Why?"

"Mmm… just wondering. "Did your father happen to leave a gift that you were to open at a certain age?"

When she squinted, he knew he was right.

"How did you know?" Her voice was laced with quiet concern.

"Just a guess. What age did he…"

"Twenty and five, but…"

"Shhh. It's of no consequence now. I'll explain everything when we reach Honorcrest." He silenced another protest with a finger to her pursed lips before helping her up into the saddle.

Four years. In four years, she would join him in transformation and together they could take to the skies. He wondered what she would think when she realized just how special she was. No wonder the Driagaran had been after her. It wasn't for the potion. They'd wanted her. Lady dragons were born only once or twice in a thousand-year period. She was rare. And she was his. Their children, their empire, combined with Kensey's and hopefully Brantley's… there would be no stopping them. Perhaps they could even defeat the Driagaran once and for all.

He sighed. It was a nice dream. Almost as nice as the one Fate had given him, he thought, looking up at the scowling lady.

The feel of a hand on his arm had him turning to where Conall stood smiling at him. When he frowned, his old friend and second in command laughed.

"You realize she has traveled through time."

Still frowning, Brendan nodded, his head bobbing up and down slowly as he tried to figure out what that had to do with anything.

Raising his brows, Conall put his hands up as if to

say *you've got to be kidding.* "Old friend. She has *traveled through time.* She has already been twenty-five." When Brendan still didn't respond, Conall rolled his eyes and tapped his hand against his own shoulder, precisely where the mark of the feather was upon the lady.

Brendan's mouth fell open with understanding. Because she had traveled through time, passing her twenty-fifth birthday, her transformation had already begun. It's why she had the mark of the feather scale. There would be no waiting four years. They needed only to get to Honorcrest where she could put on the ring her father had left her.

"What are you not telling me?" she demanded as he hauled himself up into the saddle of his destrier.

Brendan sucked in a deep breath that he exhaled slowly before he bit his bottom lip, holding it between his teeth. He closed his eyes for a split second. She'd know everything soon enough. Perhaps after seeing his men and the others transform, she'd be more willing to believe. He glanced at Conall, his old friend, nodding before giving the command that had the men spreading out a bit more to give the two the ability to talk in private.

Rynne couldn't believe what she was hearing. There was no way she could be part dragon without knowing it. Absolutely no way.

Her insides went queasy. Had Shama not told her mother that Rynne's spirit animal was a dragon? And what of Mordrin? Had the old witch not mumbled something about seeing her dragon form when she'd found the old witch the day she'd traveled into the future?

She rubbed her shoulder where the blue feather-like scale was—the mark that had fitted perfectly against Brendan's when they'd… she swallowed hard, looking away, sure her cheeks were burning at the thought of the two of them pressed so tightly together. The mark on her shoulder was blue where his was black. Did that mean she would be a black dragon since her mark had so perfectly matched his scales when he'd transformed?

No, no, no. She shook her head. This couldn't be happening. Dragons didn't exist and she certainly wasn't one.

Her chin fell to her chest, the weight of the truth on her shoulders. She knew what he was saying was the truth. She'd seen him and the others change from men to beasts and back to their human forms. Freaks of nature, she thought. Everything she'd tried to disavow, all that she had scoffed at…

Stop!

Rynne knew she'd had the visions as a child because her inner self knew her reality.

She thought of Brendan's transformation. It had looked painful. How was she to ever willingly submit her body to such brutality? She glanced at him. He seemed none the worse. In fact, he seemed almost euphoric. And the other men… they'd all transformed effortlessly. Perhaps it was just the first time.

Dear God, she thought. This couldn't be happening.

Brendan sensed Rynne's inner battle. He'd known his whole life what he was and the transformation had still been a shock. He'd known better than to fight it, but his concern for the lady's wellbeing and what she would think hadn't helped. He wished he could assure her, to find the way to lessen her fears.

He reached for her hand when he saw the moisture forming on her long lashes.

"Share your thoughts with me, my lady."

At first, she shook her head, then sucked in a deep breath. Her words were shaky when she spoke.

"Why did they not tell me? My father… he must have known."

Brendan thought for a moment, shrugging. He could only guess.

"I'm assuming they did so to keep you safe. Perhaps they felt like hiding your identity would help hide you."

"I can't believe I never knew… My own father was a dragon." Her eyes going big, she turned to him. "And my mother?"

Shaking his head, Brendan told her that wasn't very likely since she dragons were so rare.

"So… Kensey… He'll not have a dragon mate?"

Brendan could feel her sadness when he shook his head. The likelihood that her brother or Brantley would end up with true dragon mates was almost inconceivable, though their wives would have the same immortality afforded to their husbands. He told her again that she dragons were born only once or twice a century.

When one side of her mouth raised in a half smile, Brendan's brows shot up, making her laugh.

"I suppose their mates could always travel from the past or the future," she told him.

He supposed she could be right. Stranger things had happened. Was he not staring at one?

Nodding, he motioned her to follow and spurred his horse into a gallop. They had one more night before them and he wanted to make sure they spent it as far within the borders of Wolfdenreve as possible. With a little luck, they would reach Honorcrest by midday the following afternoon.

Chapter 11

Brendan paced around the guestroom at Honorcrest for the thousandth time, willing his heartbeat to slow. He wiped his palms down his sides again, taking a deep breath and counting to ten. He growled at himself, shaking out his arms before marching to the door and throwing it open.

Just get it done, he chided himself. The longer he waited to approach the lady, the more nervous he got. Even telling himself there was no way she would say no, he couldn't tamp down the fear he might hear that two-letter word. She'd been through a great deal and had fled to her room just after she'd administered the potion to Kensey and had seen that her brother was going to be all right.

The Lady Willowthorne had told him to give Rynne time, but after he'd rushed to get Kensey's blessing, he had waited as long as he could. Three days. She hadn't even come out for her brother's first flight. He'd looked for her at her window the first day the two of them took to the sky, but there'd been no hint of even a shadow behind the glass.

He hung his head. Perhaps he'd been wrong and all that he believed she had felt when they'd made love had been one-sided. Maybe the fact that he was certain Fate had brought them together made no difference to her.

Willing his feet to move faster, he trudged down the hallway toward the family wing. Either way, he had to ask. He needed to know her intent for the future.

Rynne's back was to him when he pushed open the door after she'd bid him to enter. Her head was down, and he could tell by the position of her arms that she held something in front of her. Closing the door, he took several steps toward her, stopping when she slowly turned toward him and he saw the tiny box in her hand. The sadness in her blue eyes tore at his heart like a cold, steel blade.

"I've been trying to bring myself to open it." She tried to smile. Her lips quivering, she choked back a sob instead. "What if the same thing happens to me that happened to Kensey?" She thrust the box down on the table beside her and spun away, wrapping her arms around herself. "I want to be with you, but I can't do this," she told him as he crossed the last few steps and caught her to him, her back pressed against his chest.

"Oh, love," he whispered in her ear as she melted against him. He kissed her cheek, her neck, the spot on her shoulder where the feathery image lay. "You are who you are with or without that ring. And if you're not ready to put it on, then you shouldn't." He took her hands in his when she turned around and pressed kisses to her knuckles before continuing. "Perhaps someday... Until then, I will be your strength, the one who watches over the skies above your head, doing all that I can to keep you safe and make you happy… If you'll let me."

When Rynne's eyes rounded, he smiled and took her face in his hands, brushing his lips across hers. "Did you not think I meant what I said during the night in my castle?" When she sighed, he laughed. "I would have you for all time, my lady, whether you submit to being a dragon or not. I think I have known from the moment you slogged out of my pond that there was no way I would ever let you go."

"Oh, Brendan…" she pushed her arms up around his neck, kissing him with the fervor of a love-starved whelp. "You're truly going to marry me?"

He laughed. "When we get back to Locktonhurst, I have another ring for you. It belonged to my mother, and my grandmother before her."

Rynne squealed, then sobered, pressing herself more firmly against him.

"Since we have already made this commitment, is there any reason we must wait?"

Brendan almost choked when she lifted a brow, the huskiness of her voice nearly taking his breath away, letting him know she wasn't talking about hastening the ceremony.

"It was almost unbearable to endure having you next to me those nights we slept in the forest, knowing I had to endure being robbed of your touch," she told him as she started toward her bed. "I began to believe that night in your castle must have been just a dream."

"It was a dream," he mumbled, his mouth coming down hard on hers.

Sleeping next to her without being able to slake his desires had been a task that was quite nearly beyond monumental. Now that she had agreed to be his wife and Kensey had given consent, it would be even more impossible. In his eyes, they were already united. The ceremony would take place only so that mankind could witness their union.

Chapter 12

A day later and almost an hour behind the time they'd planned to depart, Rynne finally entered the courtyard where Brendan and his men waited.

Though tight, Brendan still offered her a smile before he turned to address Conall. He was trying to be understanding, knowing how difficult it was for her to leave her family again so soon, but she'd never traveled with disgruntled, restless men who were far too ready to get home. Their patience would last only so long.

A dainty throat clearing from just behind him had Brendan turning from Conall to his wife-to-be. He raised a brow and she sighed loudly.

"How long would it take to get to Locktonhurst as the dragon flies?" she asked him.

Brendan sucked in a breath and started to speak before clamping his mouth shut. Narrowing his eyes, he looked back at his second in command and then at Rynne again. "A day, if that. Why do you ask, my lady?"

Chuckling, she opened her hand to show him the tiny dragon ring that lay in her palm. "I didn't really enjoy sleeping in the forest or the long days in the saddle." Her grin spread into a full-blown smile, her laughter ringing out when his mouth fell open.

She sobered when he grabbed her arm and steered her away from the others.

"But what of your fears?" he asked quietly, his head bent close to hers.

"I still have them. But when I saw the joy in both you and my brother when you took to the skies yesterday, and witnessed the euphoria on both of your faces when you transformed back to your human form…" She looked away and then back again. "You said yourself, whether I put the ring on or not, I am who I am… and who I am is a she dragon who has been waiting to be released for a very long time. I can feel her. The unknown is always filled with uncertainty, but, I don't want to miss out on what could be simply because I'm afraid. What if I hadn't gone to the old witch that day?" Her laugh was half-hearted. "Believe me, I was scared out of my mind. She could have just as easily turned me into a toad, or worse." She smiled when Brendan laughed.

"I'm glad you overcame your fear then, otherwise, you may not have ended up in my garden."

"Your pond, you mean."

Brendan chuckled, leaning even closer. "I swear I thought you must be a gift from the very gates of Heaven, the way you looked rising from the waters. That white dress outlining every luscious curve."

When she slapped him on the chest, he feigned hurt and they both laughed.

"You are no gentleman, Brendan MacCailín, Lord of Locktonhurst, keeper of the fiefdom of Karthmere.

You are proof that noble blood does not, in fact, make a man honorable."

Brendan raised a brow and shrugged, the playful smile never leaving his face. "Perhaps it's the dragon blood."

Rynne sobered and slowly shook her head. "Perhaps…" She looked down, opening her hand again. "How could I not have known? My own father, and the others living within the grounds of Honorcrest who were… dragons. I scorned the mythical creatures, the very thing I am, even while living amongst them." She clamped her mouth shut, grinding her teeth together as she blinked furiously, trying to hold back the tears.

Taking hold of her upper arms, Brendan turned her to face him. She leaned into the palm that he placed against her cheek.

"You weren't supposed to know. But now you do."

"Now I do," she echoed softly.

With a deep breath that she blew out loudly, she reached for his hand, turning it palm up and placing the ring in the center.

"You'll have to help me," she said, her gaze locked with his.

Brendan wished there was a way he could erase the fear he saw in her blue eyes. He'd waited his whole life for the opportunity to release his dragon, even if he hadn't imagined it happening quite the way it had. Still, he couldn't imagine not knowing who he was or living without the mental bond that had developed between himself and his dragon-form throughout the years. What turmoil Rynne must have felt. The inner conflict had to have been nearly unbearable.

And yet… she was strong, capable. She'd overcome the fear of leaving home and facing the old witch to find help for her brother. And when she'd gone through time and surfaced in his pond, even when she found herself at the tip of his sword, she'd raised her chin and pushed on, knowing her survival and her ability to get back to Honorcrest were Kensey's only hope. She hadn't backed down. She'd shown her bravery in all things; even in overcoming her hesitation to put on the ring.

With a smile, Brendan reached up and pulled the chain over his head, holding it so that the vial dangled between them.

Her eyes widening, mouth opened, Rynne cocked her head.

"You left this at Kensey's bedside," he told her.

Rynne nodded, her eyes fixed on the filled vial.

"It seems to be magic, just like you."

When she frowned, Brendan chuckled and leaned in to kiss her.

"The Raven Witch sent a message. It's not what's in the vial, love. It's you. She told me *you* are the restorer of life and health, not the liquid. Once you're wearing the ring, you'll have your full powers, but even now, because you went forward in time, you've reached the age of readiness, you're already able to heal. That's why you had to go into the future, to activate your transformation early so that you could heal your brother."

The way her eyes darted about, Brendan could tell she was trying to put all the pieces together.

"And when I tossed my coin into the fountain, I wished to go home… I did… to your home."

Brendan nodded. "To *our* home. The future you already knew exactly where you belonged."

Throwing her arms around his neck, she stood on her tiptoes, pressing feverish kisses against his lips. Brendan laughed at the way her cheeks reddened when she pulled away to hear the whoops from his men.

"Come on, Lady Katrynne. Let's make this she dragon thing official."

He led her to the center of the courtyard, motioning for the men to keep the horses back and holding out his hand for hers. As soon as she lifted it, he began to slip the gold dragon ring onto her finger.

"Relax," he told her when he saw her starting to tense. "I'll be right there by your side."

She nodded. "I have faith in you."

Brendan smiled. "As I do in you, *my* lady." Pushing the ring the rest of the way, he lifted both of her hands to kiss her fingers. "We take this leap together," he told her just before she began to transform into the most beautiful ebony dragon he had ever seen.

A single blue feather-scale blazed across her left shoulder. It perfectly matched the black one on his right shoulder when he morphed into his beast.

Lowering his head, he dropped to one front knee, his other leg extended forward in a salute to the woman who was perfectly matched to him in both human and dragon form.

Together. He heard her voice in his mind and he rose.

Together, he thought back, and with a soft flutter, they took to the skies where they were quickly greeted by those of his men who would accompany them back. The rest would have to travel back by horse, though he wasn't worried about them so much as he might have been to break up his troops before. They had received word the night before that Tamas Brantley had defeated the Driagaran trying to rescue their brethren from Garway's dungeon. In the end, it had been a bloody battle and Tamas vowed to accept help from his two neighbors from now on, especially now that they were united in wing as well as their allegiance to the King.

Chapter 13

"It's so peaceful up here."

Rynne craned her neck to look at her future husband. It was hard to believe he was a dragon shifter, even more difficult to believe she was. A week before, she had still been in denial that dragons even existed. Traveling through time will change a lot of one's beliefs, she thought, almost certain her dragon mouth had twisted itself into a smile.

"Do your people know you're a dragon?" she asked.

His grumbly snort startled her until she realized he was laughing.

"I wasn't one the last time I was there." Now they both laughed. "But they do know. Or at least they won't be surprised. My father, as you have probably already figured out, held no secret about his true self. He embraced our heritage, and I'm sure if one of his daughters was a she dragon, only the chains of a specially designed dungeon could have kept him from telling the world."

Rynne nodded, looking up when he told her that Locktonhurst was just ahead. Squinting, she could almost make out the grand castle on the cliff, her insides went giddy with anticipation.

Brendan was pleased to see his whole household turned out to greet his future bride… all except one person.

"Where is Sophia?" Brendan asked Durstan.

The old man rolled his eyes and shook his head.

"She's refusing to leave her room, my lord. Something about more feathers. Grey ones this time. Pale grey with swatches of pink and droplets of water, or some such." He threw his hands in the air and turned away. "I've given up on that one. You'll have to ask Hilde if you wish to know more. I'm only here to run your castle," he threw back as he marched off.

Rynne laughed when Brendan's chin dropped to his chest. "She'll come around, my lord. Besides, what bird has pink in its feathers? It can be none other than someone playing a joke."

Of course, Brendan thought, wishing he felt more certain. He was thinking of the black feathers that had foretold Rynne's coming. Was there any chance his sister could be a she dragon as well? That would put two of them born within a short span of each other. It couldn't be. His father would have told them.

A loud cheer erupted behind them, dragging his thoughts from his sister. They turned to see the priest's carriage laboring through the gate into the vast courtyard.

"Tis a fine thing you sent extra horses, Lord MacCailín," the portly man bellowed to him as he climbed from the rigged box. "I'm not sure my own would have made it up that hill."

Brendan extended his hand, clapping the much older man on the shoulder when he pulled him into a hug.

"I thank you for making haste, Father," he gratefully expressed, glancing up. "It looks like we're in for a bit of a squall, so I'd like to commence with the formalities as soon as possible. Karthmere weather has been known to cause too many plans to be delayed. I don't want this to be one of those times."

The old priest nodded. "Too bad you and your flighty friends can't blow it away with those big wings of yours." Several of the men laughed, as did Rynne, garnering the priest's full attention. "Ah, your lady is more beautiful than I imagined. No wonder you're in such a hurry, lad."

Rynne blushed when the priest winked at Brendan.

Hooking elbows with the two of them, he nodded toward the chapel.

"Come. Let's make this official before darkness falls and the heavens open their floodgates. I should like to be secured in your great hall by then."

"And you shall, Father. You shall. With extra ale in your belly and heavy coin in your purse."

Brendan's words brought a smile to the old man's face that shone brighter than the gold that he would be given for his services. It was almost as bright as the stars dancing in the eyes of the couple when the last words were said and the kiss was shared that would officially bind them as one.

Rynne tried to be patient as Brendan made her wait by the fireplace, her hands over her eyes. She couldn't imagine what he could be doing scurrying around his bed—*their* bed.

When she finally felt his arms go around her, she turned, snuggling against him for just a second before attempting to peek behind him. In the middle of the bed that had been stripped bare except for the bottom linen he had arranged an assortment of trinkets.

Atop crisscrossed feathers, one midnight black and one royal blue, sat a small box, its top opened to expose a ring that she could see was elegant and beguiling, even from a distance. She knew, without him telling her, that it was the ring his father had given to his mother and she couldn't help but wonder how many hundreds of years ago that had been. Wound loosely around the box was the chain of the heart-shaped vial. All of the items lay on the linen right next to the red streak from the night he'd first made love to her.

Tears wet her lashes as Rynne turned back to her husband.

"I believe you are a romantic at heart, Lord MacCailín," she told him.

Chuckling, he took her hands and started backing toward the bed.

"Shall I show you just how romantic I can be, Lady MacCailín?"

The huskiness of his voice made Rynne shiver. Knowing she was his lady sent a fire coursing through her veins, especially since she knew what was in store, having already had a taste of his romantic passion.

She giggled when he backed into the bed and fell to

the mattress, only to squeal when he pulled her down on top of him before quickly rolling her to her back. He stared down at her for a moment, her body tingling as his gaze slid over her.

She knew the sheer gown Hilde had laid out for her did little to hide her form beneath. She thought of the way he'd looked at her that first time in the garden when her wet dress may well have been as invisible as her night gown. His eyes had been cloudy with lust then. Now, the love and desire mingling in their depths nearly took her breath away.

"I love you," he whispered, covering her mouth with his. When she arched against the hand he trailed down her front, he pulled away and reached for the box containing the ring.

"For all your days, I shall love only you, my lady," he told her as he slipped the last symbol of their unity into place. It fit perfectly with the tiny dragon that already wound its way around her finger. He kissed her hand. "Dragons mate for life, you know."

Rynne nodded. Even if they hadn't been dragons, she already knew that he was hers for all eternity.

With a swiftness that echoed his need, Brendan moved the other trinkets to the stand beside the big bed, kissing her just as the first bolt of lightning cracked beyond the heavy drapes.

"I love you too," she whispered, wringing a low growl from him. When his mouth covered her breast at the same time his hand slipped beneath the silken hem of her gown and grazed her swollen sex, Rynne cried out. She'd expected this first union after their nuptial vows to be quick, but the slow movement of his fingers told her otherwise.

Rynne's body soared higher and higher, reminding her of the way she'd felt when she took to the skies in dragon form that first time. His teeth raking across her silk layered breast sent her over the edge and Rynne screamed when she felt herself falling. Floating really, like a soft feather...

Pulling Brendan's face up to hers, she wrapped her arms around his neck, her legs encircling his to guide him into her.

"Never let me go," she whispered, answering his moan with one of her own when he pressed to complete their union. His shoulder against hers burned hot where the two feather images touched.

"You asked to come home and your leap of faith delivered you to my door, because this was where you belong." He kissed her softly then began to move, driving all thoughts from her mind except for the here and now.

Home. Brendan was her home. He completed her, and no matter what lay in store for them, Rynne knew she would always find her way back to his side.

Next in the Series
A Thousand Wishes
Book 2 in A Coin in the Fountain Love Stories

Even if I had a thousand wishes…
with every single one of them, I'd still wish for you.

A castle, a coin, and an ancient fountain… the moment had all the makings for something magical to happen. Why, then, did Sophia regret her silly wish the minute the coin left her fingers? Why had she not wished for something more meaningful than coming face-to-face with the fabled ghost of the Lord of Garway Keep?

Little did she know her wish would bring far more than Lord Brantley's ghost.

Tamas Brantley stared at the dragon statue in the middle of the fountain in his outer courtyard. Kindred spirits, they were. He winked at the dragon and looked into the water. If only it would show him his future, much like a crystal ball. That's what the old witch had told him—his future was in the water.

He scoffed. Why had he felt the need to commission this fountain in the first place? Whimsey. Yes, that was why. Lady Katrynne had spoken of falling into just such a fountain and it had brought her to Brendan MacCailín, Lord of Locktonhurst. Tamas had built his in jest, saying someday maybe it would bring his lady love to him.

He turned away just as the water rippled, a lovely face rimmed with pale blonde curls replacing the translucent, glass-like surface of the pool surrounding the stone dragon.

Would the fountain grant the wishes of Sophia and Tamas? Find out in *A Thousand Wishes*, coming soon.

Stay informed at LindaBoulangerBooks.com

Or Follow Linda on her Amazon Author Page
http://www.amazon.com/Linda-Boulanger/e/B002NPYDC6

While each book in this series is a complete story about the main couple, they are all a part of something bigger: A Coin in the Fountain Love Stories Series. The books will be written/released in this order:

A Leap of Faith: Brendan and Katrynne's story
A Thousand Wishes: Tamas and Sophia's story
Love Across Time: Kensey and Isobelle's story

Author Note

I hope you enjoyed this story about Brendan and Rynne. It was originally brought to life in *The Fountain: an anthology of seven extraordinary stories* that all started with a single sentence. What a unique idea that I am so thankful to have been a part of, especially as it gave birth to a complete series for me... *A Coin in the Fountain Love Stories*, a series about the three lords mentioned in *A Leap of Faith* and their true mates who all come to them after tossing their coins into magical fountains.

If you'd like to stay informed about this series and other upcoming and new releases, promotions, giveaways, etc. first, consider following me on my Amazon author page and/or my BookBub page. They will notify you when a new book comes out, though my Facebook Group is the best place to stay in the loop. I try to interact with my members there and almost always have some sort of Members Only giveaway going Sometimes the giveaway is a free book, or an Amazon Gift Card, book swag, jewelry pieces, stuffed animals... you just never know.

You'll find that group, **Linda's Dragon Guardians, on Facebook** at this link:

https://www.facebook.com/groups/66415164041 4859/

Until the next story...
Thank you for being a part of my dream,
~Linda

Works by Linda Boulanger

Novels/Novellas
On Wings of Time
On Wings of Fire
A Leap of Faith
Stirring Up Some Love
Dance with the Enemy
Beyond the Shadows
Arms of an Angel

Novelettes
A Warrior's Christmas Gift
Makinna's Secret

Anthologies
Echoed Heartbeats
Time Out on a Roller Coaster
Becoming…
Whispered Beginnings

Color Illustrated Children's Book
When Sadie Learned to S.M.I.L.E.

Short Story Trios and Singles
Up To Bat / Center Stage / Best Friend Rules
Face of an Angel / Life Changes / Talk With Me
Secret Shame

About Linda Boulanger

Linda Boulanger is a happily-ever-after author, wife, and mother of four human children and two fur babies. She has an eclectic mix of published books, numerous story singles and short stories in a few group anthologies, plus a slew of always evolving works in progress.

Along with being an author, she designs book covers for herself and others through *Tell~Tale Book Covers* and *TreasureLine Designs*, all from her desk just north of Tulsa, Oklahoma.

Other place to find Linda:

Website
www.LindaBoulangerBooks.com

Blog
writersshelflife.blogspot.com/

Facebook
www.facebook.com/TheShelfLifeOfLindaBoulanger

Facebook Group
www.facebook.com/groups/66415164041859/

Email
lindaboulangerbooks@gmail.com

BookBub
https://www.bookbub.com/authors/linda-boulanger

Amazon Author Page
www.amazon.com/Linda-Boulanger/e/B002NPYDC6